D0112992

Karen's Baby-sitter

**Look for these
and other books about Karen
in the
Baby-sitters Little Sister series:**

Little Sister

Karen's Baby-sitter
Ann M. Martin

Illustrations by Susan Tang

A
LITTLE APPLE
PAPERBACK

SCHOLASTIC INC.
New York Toronto London Auckland Sydney

If you purchased this book without a cover, you should be aware that this book is stolen property. It was reported as "unsold and destroyed" to the publisher, and neither the author nor the publisher has received any payment for this "stripped book."

No part of this publication may be reproduced in whole or in part, or stored in a retrieval system, or transmitted in any form or by any means, electronic, mechanical, photocopying, recording, or otherwise, without written permission of the publisher. For information regarding permission, write to Scholastic Inc., 555 Broadway, New York, NY 10012.

ISBN 0-590-47045-0

Copyright © 1994 by Ann M. Martin. All rights reserved. Published by Scholastic Inc. APPLE PAPERBACKS ® and BABY-SITTERS LITTLE SISTER ® are registered trademarks of Scholastic Inc.

12 11 10 9 8 7   9/9

Printed in the U.S.A.   40

First Scholastic printing, February 1994

Karen's Baby-sitter

1

The Carpenter

"Uh-oh," said Seth. "I left some papers at my workshop. I will have to go get them. I need them tonight."

Seth Engle is my stepfather. He is a carpenter. I did not know why he needed those papers so badly, but I wanted to go with him to get them. I just love his workshop.

I am Karen Brewer. I am seven years old. This is what I look like: freckles, blue eyes, long blonde hair. Also, I wear glasses. I have two pairs. The blue pair is for reading.

The pink pair is for the rest of the time. (Except for when I am asleep. Or in the bathtub.)

"Seth, can I come with you? Puh-*lease*?" I begged.

"Me too?" said Andrew. "Can I come, too?"

Andrew is my little brother. He is four going on five. I do not know why he always wants to do what I want to do.

It was already after dinner. Seth looked at his watch. "Karen?" he said. "Do you have any homework?"

"I already finished it," I replied.

"Andrew, do you need a bath?"

"I took one last night," Andrew replied.

"Okay, then you may come with me."

"Thank you!" Andrew and I cried.

We said good-bye to Mommy. We piled into the car. Seth drove through the cold, dark night. Our teeth chattered until the heater warmed up the car.

Soon Seth parked in back of his workshop. The workshop is downtown in Sto-

2

neybrook. (Stoneybrook is the town we live in. It is in Connecticut.) Seth's workshop sits next to a parking lot behind a row of stores. It is divided into two rooms. The little room is the office. The big room is where Seth makes furniture and kitchen cabinets.

Andrew and I hurried into the workshop behind Seth. For a moment we just stood and looked at everything. We saw hammers and saws and lots of other tools. We saw jars full of nails and screws in all sizes. We saw big pieces of equipment we are not allowed to touch. We saw the floor. The floor is always a mess. That night it was covered with curly wood shavings. And, of course, everywhere Andrew and I looked we saw wood — boards and planks and long strips of molding, balsa wood as light as a feather, and pieces of cherry and mahogany I could hardly lift.

"Seth, could I collect some stuff for my collage?" I asked. (I am working on a collage. I need all different kinds of materials to glue to it. Those wood shavings looked very interesting.)

"Sure," Seth answered. "Just be careful." When Seth says that, he means do not go near anything sharp.

I wandered around the workshop. I collected shavings and little sawed-off ends of molding. Andrew helped me. Seth searched through the desk in his office. He was looking for the papers. After awhile he looked in the files near Ruth's desk. Ruth is the woman who runs the office for Seth. I like her. She has worked with Seth for a long time.

Andrew and I finished collecting stuff. We looked at the things Seth was building — beds and tables and cabinets and bookcases. Finally Seth found the papers he wanted.

"Time to go, kids!" he called.

We rode home through the quiet streets. My brother and I fell asleep before we reached our house.

2

Offices

I like seeing where my parents work. I especially like offices. I like copier machines and pencils and markers. At Elizabeth's office, I know how to operate the fax machine. (Elizabeth is my stepmother.) In fact, I know how to operate a lot of things. That is because I can go to *three* different offices — Seth's office, Daddy's office, and Elizabeth's office. (Mommy does not go to an office, except sometimes to Seth's.)

See, I have two families. A long time ago, when I was just a little kid, I had only one family — Mommy, Daddy, Andrew, and me. We lived together in a very big house, the house Daddy grew up in. I thought we were happy, but I guess we were not. Mommy and Daddy began to fight. A lot. Loudly. Finally they said they were going to get a divorce. They said they loved Andrew and me very much, but they did not love each other anymore. And they did not want to live together.

So Mommy moved out of the big house. She took Andrew and me with her. We moved into a little house. The houses are not too far away from each other. Now Andrew and I live at Daddy's big house every other weekend and on some vacations and holidays. We live at Mommy's little house the rest of the time. And we belong to two families, since Mommy and Daddy have each gotten married again. Mommy married Seth, our stepfather. Daddy married Elizabeth, our stepmother. These are the people in our two families:

At the little house are Mommy, Seth, Andrew, and me. Oh, and Rocky, Midgie, and Emily Junior. Rocky and Midgie are Seth's cat and dog. Emily Junior is my rat.

At the big house are (get ready) Daddy, Elizabeth, Andrew, me, Kristy, Sam, Charlie, David Michael, Emily Michelle, and Nannie. And our pets — Shannon, Boo-Boo, Goldfishie, and Crystal Light the Second. I better explain who everybody is. Kristy, Sam, Charlie, and David Michael are Elizabeth's kids. (She was married once before she married Daddy.) So they are my stepsister and stepbrothers. Kristy is thirteen. She is an excellent baby-sitter. She is also one of my favorite people. Sam and Charlie are old. They go to high school. David Michael is seven like me, but he is not in my class. That is because he does not go to my school. I go to Stoneybrook Academy. He goes to Stoneybrook Elementary. Emily Michelle is my adopted sister. She is two and a half years old. Daddy and Elizabeth adopted her from the faraway country of Vietnam. (I named my rat after

8

her.) Nannie is Elizabeth's mother, so she is my stepgrandmother. She helps take care of us and the house and the pets. Shannon is David Michael's puppy. Boo-Boo is Daddy's cross old cat. Guess what Goldfishie and Crystal Light are.

I made up special nicknames for my brother and me. I call us Andrew Two-Two and Karen Two-Two. (I thought up those names after my teacher read aloud a book called *Jacob Two-Two Meets the Hooded Fang*.) We are two-twos because we have two houses and two families, two mommies and two daddies, two cats and two dogs. Plus we have clothes and books and toys at the little house, and other clothes and books and toys at the big house. That is so we do not have to pack much when we go back and forth. I even have two best friends. And of course I have those two pairs of glasses.

Being a two-two is not bad. Except that I wish I could spend more time with Daddy and my big-house family.

3

Bart

Mostly I only get to see Daddy and my big-house family every other weekend. That is not enough. I *love* the big house. It is noisy and busy and bursting with people. Just the way I like things. Plus, one of my best friends lives across the street. My best friends are Hannie Papadakis and Nancy Dawes. Hannie is the one who lives across from the big house. Nancy lives next door to the little house. Hannie and Nancy and I are all in Ms. Colman's second-grade class. We call ourselves the Three Muske-teers.

One snowy Saturday, Andrew and I were at the big house. So far, it had been a great day. Six inches of new snow were on the ground when we woke up that morning. Daddy made pancakes for breakfast. Charlie let us help him shovel the driveway. Sam let us turn on the snowblower. (My two big brothers have a snow shoveling business. Once, I tried to help them run it. But mostly I just got us all in trouble.) When we had finished shoveling our driveway, Nannie had made us hot chocolate. Now it was after lunch. Andrew and I were playing outside again. David Michael was with us.

"Hi! Hi, you guys!" someone called. It was Hannie. She was pulling her sled across the street.

"Hi!" I called back. "Come help us. We are going to build a snow fort!"

Hannie and my brothers and I began digging around in the snow. We had plenty of snow to dig in. A lot of snow had already been on the ground before the new snow fell. We made tunnels. We made rooms. We packed the snow tightly.

After awhile, I stood back. "You know," I said, looking at our work, "the fort is . . . not great."

"Yikes!" shrieked David Michael. "You are not kidding. Half of it just fell on me!"

"Need some help?"

I turned around. There was Kristy. She was coming out the door with Bart Taylor. Bart is Kristy's friend. And he is a boy. But I am not sure if he is her boyfriend.

"Yes!" I called. "We do need help."

"Our fort is collapsing," said David Michael. He brushed some snow off of his hat and sleeves.

"Let's take a look," said Bart.

He and Kristy crawled around our fort.

"We wanted it to have a roof," I said.

"And windows," added Andrew.

Bart and Kristy began to pile up the snow. "You have to start with a big moun-

12

tain," said Bart. "A mountain of snow. And then tunnel inside it, like this."

Soon my friends and I were digging and tunneling and packing the snow. Bart and Kristy helped us make an igloo fort. It had three rooms and two windows and a doorway.

"Cool," said Hannie as we stood back to look at the fort.

"This is our best fort ever," I added.

"I'll say," said David Michael.

"You know what you can do to the fort?" said Bart. "Later today, when you are ready to stop playing, pour cold water — very carefully — on the fort. Then it will freeze. Tomorrow the fort will be ice-covered. It will last longer."

"It will be glittery, too," I said. "A fairy princess castle."

David Michael made a face, but I did not care. Anyway, I could tell he thought Bart was as wonderful as I did. So did Andrew and Hannie. Bart had made our day in the snow perfect.

14

4

Ruth's Emergency

Late on Sunday afternoon, just before dinnertime, Daddy drove Andrew and me back to the little house.

"Good-bye!" I called. "I wish we could stay longer."

"So do I, pumpkin," said Daddy. "I'll see you in two weeks."

"See you in two weeks," echoed Andrew sadly.

My brother and I ran inside. "Mommy!" we shouted. "Seth!"

Mommy dashed into the hallway to meet

us. "Shhh! Hi, you two," she whispered loudly. "Seth is on the telephone. Keep your voices down," she added.

"Why? What is wrong?" I asked.

"Who is Seth talking to?" asked Andrew.

"He's talking to Ruth," Mommy replied. "From the office. She is very upset. I am not sure what happened."

We had to wait until Seth got off the phone to find out.

"Hi, kids," said Seth tiredly when he had hung up. Then he turned to Mommy. "Well, that was Ruth," he said. "I guess you could tell. She just found out that her mother needs to have an operation. It is not an emergency — the surgery is scheduled for next week — but it is serious. Ruth wants to fly to Canada to stay with her parents for two weeks. She wants to leave next Saturday. Of course she is worried about her mother. She is also worried about the office. And so am I. We are very busy right now. I need help. I have to fill a lot of orders."

16

"Could you hire a temporary secretary?" asked Mommy. "Just for two weeks?"

"I suppose so," replied Seth. "But I really need someone who knows the business."

"Well," said Mommy, grinning, "what about me? I have worked in the office before. I know the business pretty well."

Seth grinned, too. "That would be terrific, honey. But what about the kids? Who would watch them when they are not in school?"

Mommy frowned. "That *is* a problem."

I did not think so. "I know!" I said. "Call Kristy! She can baby-sit for us. Please? We love Kristy."

"I am not sure if she can come every day for two weeks," said Mommy. "That is a big job." Even so, the next day, Mommy called Kristy at her meeting of the Baby-sitters Club. She asked if Kristy or one of her friends could baby-sit for Andrew and me. Guess what. They wanted to take the job, but they could not. They were very busy. Nobody was free for two whole weeks. But Kristy had an idea.

"What about calling my friend Bart Taylor?" she suggested. "He has not done much baby-sitting. But he is great with children. He even coaches a softball team for little kids in his neighborhood. Plus, he lives near you. Right in between our house and yours. He could walk to your house and back."

When Mommy asked Andrew and me about Bart, we shrieked, "Call him! Call him! Call him! We love Bart!"

"As much as you love Kristy?" asked Mommy. She was smiling.

"Almost as much," I said.

Mommy called Bart. He took the job. He said he would be happy to baby-sit for my brother and me. So this is what Mommy and Seth and Bart worked out: Every day while Ruth was away, Mommy would take Andrew and me to school in the morning. Then she would go to Seth's office to work. At lunchtime, she would pick up Andrew at his preschool, bring him home, and wait

18

for me to come home from school later. After Bart came over, she would go back to Seth's office and work there until dinner-time. I thought this sounded exciting. I was sorry Ruth's mother was sick. But I could not wait for my new baby-sitter.

Karen's Baby-sitter

*D*ing-dong!

"I'll get it!" I shrieked. It was Monday afternoon. Nancy's mother had just driven me home from school. Now our doorbell was ringing.

"Indoor voice, Karen," said Mommy. "Please calm down."

"But it is Bart!" I cried. "Bart is here! I know he is."

Sure enough, Bart was standing at our front door.

"Hi! Come on inside!" I told him.

I was ready to play with Bart, but Mommy wanted to talk to him first. "The important phone numbers are posted here by the phone," said Mommy. She led Bart into the kitchen. "Here is the number of the office where you can reach Mr. Engle and me. Here is the number of the children's doctor. And here are other emergency numbers. Now don't let the kids eat too much, okay? Mr. Engle and I will be home by six, and we will give the kids dinner then."

"Okay," said Bart.

I could not wait for Mommy to leave. Even though the weather was yucky and we would have to stay inside, I knew we would have fun.

I was right. Bart let us do anything we wanted to do.

"Can we make a cave?" asked Andrew.

"Sure," replied Bart. He paused. "Um, how do you make a cave?"

"With a card table and blankets and the couch," replied Andrew.

We lugged a card table into the living room. We set it up next to the couch. Then we spread blankets over the back of the couch and across the top of the table. We let them hang down the sides. We had made a two-room cave. We fit inside it nicely.

"Let's be bears," said Andrew.

We growled around for awhile. Then we pretended we were hibernating, but that was boring.

"Okay, we will be tickle bears!" said Bart.

Bart tickled Andrew and me. We laughed and squirmed so much we knocked the table over.

"Uh-oh," said Andrew.

But Bart did not seem to care about the table. He leaped up and cried, "Tickle bear tag!" He chased Andrew and me out of the living room and through the hallway. As he passed by a plant stand, he almost knocked it over. But he caught it in time. That was lucky. Mommy's favorite plant sits on that stand. It's a fern named Miss Fern, in a very beautiful china pot. If the stand had fallen over, the pot would have smashed, and Miss Fern would not have been a happy plant. Mommy would not have been happy either.

"Whew," said Bart. "That was close."

"Hey, can we bake brownies?" I wanted to know.

"Do you have brownie mix?" asked Bart.

"I think so."

We looked in the kitchen and found the mix. And we had everything else we needed to bake brownies. "Goody!" I exclaimed.

"Can I stir up the ingrediments?" asked Andrew.

"Ingredients," I corrected him.

"Sure," said Bart.

Bart did not care when Andrew dropped the goopy spoon on the floor. He did not care when I got chocolate in my hair, either. By the time Mommy and Seth came home,

the kitchen was a big mess. (So was the living room.) But the brownies were ready and waiting.

Mommy and Seth and Andrew and I ate them for dessert that night.

6

The Winter Olympics

On Tuesday, Bart came over again. This time the weather was nice. (Well, nice for the middle of winter.) It was sunny and cold, but not too cold. And three inches of new snow lay on the ground.

"Puh-lease can we play outside?" Andrew asked Bart.

"Gigundo please?" I added.

Not all baby-sitters like to take kids outside to play in the snow. We need a long time to bundle up. Then sometimes, as soon as we are bundled up, we have to take

everything off so we can go to the bathroom. But Bart did not mind bundling us
up. Even Andrew, who has to put his
clothes on in a certain order, or else he
throws a tantrum.

Andrew and I put on extra socks. We
slipped plastic bags over the socks (to keep
our feet dry in case any snow got in our
boots). Then we put on sweaters, jackets,
snow pants, boots, hats, scarves, and two
pairs of mittens each. When we were ready,
I looked at Andrew. "Do you have to go to
the bathroom?" I asked him.

"Nope," he answered. "Do you?"

"Nope," I replied. (I was surprised.)

Bart and Andrew and I stood in our back-
yard. "You know what?" said Bart. "Your
yard is perfect for sledding."

"It *is*?" I said. "But we do not have a
hill."

"You have a slope," said Bart. "And that
is perfect."

Bart showed us how to trample down a
track for sledding. He started at the highest

point in our yard. Then *stamp, stamp, stamp.*
He stamped a path from there down to the
lowest part. He packed the snow with his
boots. Andrew and I followed him, stamp-
ing, too. After that, Bart added some snow
to the higher part, making it even higher.
Then he stamped the new snow down.

We stood back to admire our sledding
track.

"Now," said Bart, "what do you have to
sled on besides a sled? We do not want
anything with runners. The runners will
ruin the track."

"We have a saucer," said Andrew.

"And a toboggan," I added.

"Great," said Bart. "Did you know you
can even use a tray?" He found an old tray
in the kitchen and brought that outside,
too.

We had been sliding on the track for
about ten minutes when Nancy came over.
She brought her new pink saucer.

"Cool sledding track!" she said.

Pretty soon Kathryn and Willie came

over. (They live across the street.) They brought their toboggan. A few minutes later Bobby Gianelli came over with his sled. Now here is the thing about Bobby. He is also in Ms. Colman's class with Nancy and me. And he is a *bully*.

I ran to Bart. I tugged at his sleeve. "Bart, *Bobby* is here. He is going to ruin everything. He — "

"He just wants to play, Karen," said Bart.

"But he brought his *sled*. It has *run*ners. You said no runners."

Bart cleared his throat. "Attention! Attention, please!" he cried. Andrew and Nancy and Kathryn and Willie and Bobby and I gathered around Bart. "We will now hold the Winter Olympics," Bart went on. "The first event is the two-person toboggan race."

All afternoon we slid around our yard. Bart made up one event after another for the Olympics. Bobby's sled was not used in a single one. So Bobby could not ruin our track with his runners.

By the time Mommy and Seth came home, our friends had left. We had taken our things off and left them in a pile by the back door. Seth and Mommy looked at the pile (and at some puddles nearby), but they did not say anything.

7

Bermuda

When Bart left our house, Mommy and Seth made dinner. They warmed up a big pot of vegetable stew. That was the perfect dinner. Andrew and I were cold because we had been playing in the snow. The stew warmed us up. Also, Andrew and I traded vegetables. He gave me his carrots and I gave him my cauliflower.

After dinner, I decided to work on my collage. I sat at the table in my room. I spread out the stuff I had collected. Then I looked at the things I had already glued onto a sheet of oaktag — some sequins, four noodles (not cooked), some scraps of velvet, and a patch of glitter (blue and green).

"Hmm," I said to myself. "What this collage needs is pictures."

I ran downstairs. I found a stack of newspapers that we were going to recycle. I took one of them back to my room with me.

"Now let me see," I said. "Here is a picture of a man giving an award to a woman. That is not very interesting. And here is a picture of a building. That is not very interest— Oh, here is a picture of a dog and a cat who are best friends. Now *that* will be good for the collage."

I cut out the picture. Then I found one of a girl planting a tree. I cut that out, too. I turned a page in the paper. And there, spread across two whole pages was a beautiful color picture of a beach. (All the other pictures were black and white.)

"Ooh," I said softly.

In the picture, a man and a woman and two children were walking along a beach. The sand was white. The water behind them was bright blue. So was the sky. The people in the family were wearing their bathing suits. The kids were holding seashells. One of them was pointing to a palm tree. They were laughing.

The writing at the top of these pages read: *DO YOU HAVE THE WINTER BLAHS? WIN A TRIP TO BERMUDA! VISIT THE ISLAND OF YOUR DREAMS.*

I would not mind going to Bermuda, I thought. Snow is fun, but I bet the beach would be fun right now, too. I imagined myself walking along the sand with that family, looking for seashells. Then I imagined myself sailing in a little boat on the water. Then I imagined Bart there with me. I bet Bart could make Bermuda really fun. He would think of great games to play on the beach. And he would probably know

how to make gigundoly wonderful sand castles.

I began to cut out the picture of the palm tree. It would look perfect on my collage. But suddenly I stopped. I had thought of something. *I* should enter the contest. If I won, then I really could go to Bermuda with Bart.

I read the ad for the contest. The contest was being held by a store in Stoneybrook. The winner would be chosen soon, but I still had time to enter. The trip to Bermuda was the grand prize. There was a first prize and then there were some second and third prizes, too. But I did not care about them. I just wanted to go to Bermuda.

At the bottom of the ad was a coupon to fill out. I was about to write down my name and address when I saw some teeny-tiny writing. It said: *Must be eighteen or older to enter.* Well, that was pretty silly. A person did not have to be eighteen to know how to fill out that form. I am only seven, and I know how to write my name and address.

So I did. Then I cut out the form and put it in an envelope. I would mail it the next day.

I crossed my fingers for good luck. Then I worked on my collage some more.

8

The Incredible Journey

On Wednesday, Bart was our baby-sitter again.

When he rang the bell, I let him inside.

"Hi, guys!" said Bart. He took off his coat. Then he almost knocked over that plant stand again. (Bart has awfully long legs. I heard Mommy say he is gangly. I wonder if that means clumsy.) Anyway, luckily for Miss Fern, I caught the stand just in time.

"Whoa, thanks," said Bart. "Sorry, plant."

"Her name is Miss Fern," I told him.

"Sorry, Miss Fern."

Mommy said Bart and Andrew and I could have a snack. So after she left we got out the brownies we had baked. We ate them with milk. That is really the only way to enjoy a brownie.

"So, you guys. What's going on?" asked Bart.

"Not much," replied Andrew.

"I am making a collage," I said.

"Cool," said Bart. He paused. "What are you doing this weekend?"

Andrew smiled. "I am going to a birthday party!" he said proudly. "Saturday is Greg's party and he is turning five. A magician is coming. Greg said he is going to pull handkerchiefs out of his mouth."

"Gross," I said.

"Decent," Bart said. "Karen, what are you doing this weekend?"

I shrugged. "I don't know. I did not make any plans. Maybe I will work on the collage."

"Do you want to come over to my house on Saturday?" asked Bart. "I am going to rent a video. It is an old movie called *The Incredible Journey*. I think you would like it. It is about two dogs and a cat who travel all the way across country to find their owners."

I was hardly listening to Bart. I could not believe what he had just said. He had invited me to his house. He had asked me for a *date*.

"So do you want to come over?" said Bart again.

"Sure!" I exclaimed. I wanted to do anything Bart wanted to do.

After we finished our snack, I ran to my room. I needed to think for a few minutes. I wanted to hug the happy news to myself. But while I was thinking I thought of a problem. How could I go on a date? I am already married. I have a husband named Ricky Torres.

9

Karen's Dream Date

In case you could not tell, I am not *really* married. Ricky Torres is my pretend husband. We got married on the playground at school one day. Ricky is in Ms. Colman's class with Nancy and Hannie and me. And he got glasses at the same time I did. I think that is why we became friends. Anyway, later we decided to hold a wedding and get married. He has been my pretend husband ever since.

I wondered how Ricky would feel if he knew Bart had asked me for a date. I wondered how he would feel if he knew how badly I wanted to go on the date. I decided to try not to think about it.

When Mommy and Seth came home from work on Wednesday night, I told them Bart had invited me to his house to see a movie on Saturday. (I did not tell them he had asked me for a date, though. That was my own special secret.) Anyway, Mommy said I could go.

"Yes!" I cried.

On Thursday morning I could not wait to arrive at school. I wanted to see Hannie and Nancy. When I did, I whispered to them, "I have very exciting news. Let's have a meeting on the playground today." (When Hannie and Nancy and I have news to share, we usually gather under a big tree at recess, and hold a meeting, just the three of us.)

"What is your news?" asked Hannie as soon as we were standing under the tree. She was so excited she was jumping up and down.

"Well," I said slowly, "you will not believe this — "

"Just *tell* us, Karen!" cried Nancy.

"Okay. Bart Taylor asked me for a date. And I think I am in love with him. Oh, I could just faint," I added.

Nancy and Hannie began talking at the same time.

"I thought you were in love with Ricky," said Nancy.

"Yeah, he is your husband," said Hannie.

"I remember when I was in love with Mr. Howard," said Nancy. (Mr. Howard was a student teacher. He does not teach our class anymore.)

"What about Kristy?" asked Hannie. "Isn't Bart Kristy's boyfriend?"

"What kind of date?" asked Nancy.

"Where are you going?" asked Hannie.

I did not know what to say first. Finally I told my friends about the date. "Bart invited me over to his house to watch a movie," I said. *"The Incredible Journey*. It's an animal story."

"Cool," said Hannie and Nancy.

"And I do not know about Kristy and Bart. I do not really think Bart is Kristy's boyfriend. I think maybe he is just a friend who is a boy. Also," I went on, "Ricky is my pre*tend* husband. He knows that. Now help me plan for my date, you guys."

"Okay," said Nancy. "When is the date?"

"On Saturday afternoon," I replied.

"What are you going to wear?" asked Hannie.

"My pink-and-white-striped dress. Do you think I should bring anything to Bart?" I wondered.

"A corsage," said Nancy. "That is what girls give boys on dates."

"A corsage," I repeated. "A flower. Okay."

"And you have to act grown-up," added

Hannie. "Do not mention second grade or Barbie or snowmen."

"All right," I said. And then I told my friends about the contest and about winning the Winter Blahs Trip to Bermuda. "Going to Bermuda with Bart," I said, "would be my dream date."

10

The Mess

Thursday was another fun day with Bart. The sun was shining, so Kathryn and Willie and Bobby and Nancy came over. We held another Winter Olympics. But on Friday, the weather was yucky. The sky was gray, and sleet was falling. It stung my cold cheeks as I ran into the little house after school.

"Boo," I said. "Boo and bullfrogs. Now we cannot play outside with Bart." But that did not matter. When Bart came over, he had more fun ideas for things to do indoors.

And then, just as we were about to start a game, the doorbell rang.

"I'll get it!" I yelled. (Bart did not tell me to use my indoor voice. He just followed me to the door.)

Nancy was standing on the porch, shivering in the sleet. "I came over to play," she said. "Maybe we could have the *Indoor* Winter Olympics today." She stepped inside.

Nancy had not even finished taking off her things when the bell rang again. There were Kathryn and Willie. Soon the doorbell rang a third time. Bully Bobby had come over. I could not believe it.

I looked at Bart in dismay. But all he said was, "The first event in the Indoor Winter Olympics will be bowling."

"Bowling!" I exclaimed. "We do not have enough room for bowling."

"Yes, you do. You have a staircase," said Bart.

Bart looked around our kitchen. He

found ten plastic water bottles. Seth had put them in a paper bag to be recycled. Now Bart set up the bottles on the first four steps of our staircase. Andrew and my friends and I were waiting at the top of the stairs. When Bart was finished, he climbed the steps. He handed each of us a ball. "Now what you do is sit on the top step and drop your ball down the stairs. See how many bottles you can knock over."

Andrew went first. He threw his ball too hard. It hit the middle step, bounced, and crashed onto a table down in the living room. (Nothing broke.)

"Next time, *drop* the ball," said Bart. "Don't throw it."

Nancy went next. She dropped her ball carefully, and it knocked over six bottles. Also it got lost downstairs. Bart went looking for it. As he ran through the hallway, he passed by Miss Fern. He knocked into the plant stand, but it did not fall over.

"Sorry, Miss Fern," said Bart.

When we had had enough bowling, Bart made us snacks. He put cheese and tomato slices on crackers. Then he stuck them in the microwave. He called them Cracker Pizzas. We left cracker crumbs and tomato goo all over the kitchen. The crumbs crunched under our feet. Bart said we could clean up the mess later, but he forgot.

Soon the sky grew dark. Our friends went home. A little later, Mommy and Seth came back.

"Hi!" Andrew and I cried.

"Hi . . ." Mommy was looking around. She looked at the bottles and balls on the living room floor. She looked at the crumbs and the tomato goo in the kitchen. "Bart?" she said.

"Yes?" replied Bart.

"I really must ask you to keep the house neater from now on. Seth and I do not like returning to such a mess every day."

Yipes! Mommy was scolding Bart! I could not believe it.

But Bart did not seem upset. He said, "Sorry, Mrs. Engle. Sorry, Mr. Engle. I will try to be neater next week."

"Thank you," replied Mommy. "We would appreciate that."

11

Bart's Lie

The next day was Saturday. Andrew was off to the birthday party. "Good-bye!" he called to me as he and Mommy climbed into the car. "When I come back I will have a goody bag — and I'm not sharing!"

"I would not *want* anything from your goody bag," I replied. "It would be all covered with cooties."

"That is enough, you two," said Mommy.

After Andrew left I ran to my room to get dressed. I put on the pink-and-white dress. Then I pulled on white tights, and buckled on my tappy black party shoes. I tied a ribbon in my hair.

"Now for Bart's corsage," I said. On my dresser was a cardboard box. I peeked inside. In it I had put a red plastic rose. I had found the rose with my collage stuff. I had placed it on a lovely bed of blue tissue paper.

I ran downstairs and put on my coat and boots and hat and mittens. "Ready!" I called to Seth. "I am ready to go!"

Seth drove me to Bart's house. I carried the corsage box in my lap. When we reached the Taylors' I asked Seth if I could go to the door by myself. Nancy and Hannie and I had agreed that waiting at the door by myself would look much more grown-up than standing there with an adult. Seth let me go. (But he waited in the car until he saw Bart.)

"Good afternoon, Bart," I said when he opened the door.

"Hi, Karen," he replied.

I stepped inside and looked around. Bart's home seemed like most other houses — except, of course, that it was *Bart's*. That made it special.

I held out the box to Bart. "This is for you," I said. I was beginning to wonder where Bart was going to put the corsage. A corsage is supposed to be pinned to a person's jacket. But Bart was not wearing a jacket. In fact, he was not very dressed up at all. Wasn't our date important to him?

"A present for me?" said Bart. He opened the box. "This is . . . this is really nice, Karen. Um, what is it?"

"It is a cor*sage*," I replied.

"Oh!" Bart sounded surprised. "Well, I will wear it later, I guess. Come on in the TV room, Karen. Everyone is here."

Everyone? Who else was coming on our date?

I took off my coat and boots and hat and mittens. Bart led me down a hallway and into a small room. I looked inside. I saw Kristy and David Michael.

"Hi!" called Kristy. "Glad you could come, Karen."

I opened my mouth. I closed it again. What were Kristy and David Michael doing there? I began to have a funny feeling about my date. Especially since Kristy and David Michael were not any more dressed up than Bart was. They were wearing jeans and sweat shirts. I was the only person dressed for a party date.

"Okay, let's start the movie," said Bart. He popped it in the VCR. Then he sat on the couch. He sat next to Kristy. And he took her hand. Bart held Kristy's hand during the entire movie. He never let go of it. (He was supposed to be holding *my* hand.)

I could not tell you whether the movie was any good. I do not remember a thing about it. The only thing I do remember is sitting on the floor with David Michael. We were the children, and Bart and Kristy were the big people. At least, that is how I felt.

I tried not to talk to anybody.

I could not wait for Seth to come pick me up.

When I got home, I ran to my room. I flumped down on my bed. I was gigundoly sad. Bart was mean. He had *lied* to me.

I was too embarrassed to tell anyone what had happened.

12

Mean Bart

On Sunday, I hardly spoke to anyone. Mostly I stayed in my bedroom. Mommy thought I was coming down with a cold. She was wrong. I was not sick, I was dying. I was dying of a broken heart.

Guess what. By Monday I was not sad anymore. I was mad. Mad at Bart. When he rang the bell that afternoon, I let Andrew answer the door.

"Hi, Bart! Hi, Bart!" I heard Andrew cry. Andrew sounded very excited to see Bart. Too bad he did not know better.

When Mommy left, Bart and Andrew sat down at the kitchen table for a snack. "Come join us, Karen," said Bart.

"No, thank you," I replied. I plopped in front of the TV. I stared at it for awhile.

Soon I heard Bart say, "Okay, Andrew. We have to clean up the kitchen before we play outside."

Ha. Now I was glad Mommy had scolded Bart about leaving messes. Bart deserved to be scolded. He was a *mean* person.

After Bart had cleaned up the kitchen, he said to me, "Andrew and I have decided to play outside. We are going to start the Winter Olympics again."

"I do not want to play," I told him.

"Well, I cannot leave you inside," said Bart.

I sighed very loudly. "Oh, all right." I stood up. I put on my snow clothes. When Bart tried to help me with my scarf, I jerked away from him. "I can do it myself," I told him.

"Karen?" said Bart. "Is something — "

I did not let him finish his sentence. "Come on, Andrew," I said. "Do not be a slowpoke. Let's go."

But when we got outside, I sat on the front stoop. I let Andrew and Bart run into the yard. I was not going to play with them no matter what. (Well, I was not going to play with Bart.)

I wished I could go over to the Daweses' house and play with Nancy. But I couldn't. The Daweses were not at home.

After awhile, Bully Bobby came over. When Andrew saw him, he said, "I will go get Willie and Kathryn. We need them for the Olympics, too."

Soon Andrew and Bobby and Kathryn and Willie were running around. "Come play with us, Karen!" called Andrew. "We need *more* people for the Olympics."

"No, thank you!" I called back.

"Pleeeease?"

"I said no, thank you."

Andrew stuck his tongue out at me. I ignored him.

Later, when the kids were busy seeing who could throw a snowball the farthest, Bart sat next to me on the stoop.

"What is wrong, Karen?" he asked.

"Nothing."

"Are you sure? Because — "

"I said nothing is wrong."

"Okay."

Bart left me alone after that. When our friends went home, Andrew and Bart and I went inside. But this time, Bart was smart. He asked us to take our boots off at the door so we would not make puddles in the house. Then he hung up our clothes instead of leaving them in a pile on the floor. After that he checked the kitchen and the living room to make sure we had not left any messes.

When Mommy and Seth came home they looked very happy. They smiled at Bart.

"Good job," said Seth.

Bart smiled back.

13

Getting Even

On Tuesday morning, I woke up feeling grumbly. I realized I was *still* mad at Bart.

Grumble, grumble, grumble. I was rude to Mommy at breakfast. I snapped at Andrew when he asked me to help him put his boots on. On the way to school, I sat in the car with my arms folded. I did not say a word to Seth.

But when I saw Hannie and Nancy in Ms. Colman's room, I decided I needed to talk to somebody. I needed my two best friends.

"You guys?" I said. "Can I talk to you?"

"Sure," they answered.

"Remember what I said when you asked me how my date with Bart was?"

"You said it was fine," replied Hannie.

I nodded. "But that was not true. I kind of told a lie. The date was awful, but I was too embarrassed to say so."

"It was awful?" repeated Nancy. "What happened?"

I sighed. "Bart invited other people on our date. He invited Kristy and David Michael. They watched the movie with us, too. And Bart and Kristy sat together and held hands. I sat on the floor with David Michael. Plus, no one else was dressed up. I was the only person wearing party clothes. Bart lied about our date."

"Oh, Karen," said Nancy. "That is too bad."

"Too bad," echoed Hannie.

"I know," I replied.

"Bart must be a creep," said Nancy.

"A jerk," said Hannie.

"Thank goodness for my husband," I went on. "Ricky would never do something like that to me. Now I know why I married him."

"What are you going to do about Bart?" asked Hannie.

My answer was ready. "Get even," I replied.

"How?" Nancy wanted to know.

"That is what we have to figure out," I said. "I need you to help me. But I do not think we have time to do that right now. Ms. Colman will be here any minute. Let's have a meeting on the playground again."

So that is what we did. After lunch, we gathered at our tree. In the warm weather, we can sit on the ground under the tree. Sometimes we climb its branches. But that Tuesday was cold and snowy, so we just stood by the tree trunk and talked.

"Okay," began Hannie. "What do you want to do to Bart?"

"Embarrass him," I replied. "That is what he did to me."

"Hmm," said Nancy. "You mean like make his pants fall down?"

My friends and I giggled. "I guess so," I said. "That would be embarrassing, all right. Especially if a lot of people saw. But I do not know how I could make his pants fall down."

"Well then, you could trip him," suggested Hannie. "That is always embarrassing."

I wrinkled my nose. "Not embarrassing enough, though."

We thought for a few minutes. "Okay," said Nancy finally. "What kinds of things embarrass Bart?"

"Well . . . I think he was embarrassed when Mommy told him he was a sloppy baby-sitter. She had to ask him to keep the house neater while he is in charge," I said.

Hannie and Nancy frowned. I could tell they were not getting any ideas. But I was getting one. A good idea. A good and mean idea.

"I know!" I cried. "I know just the thing!"

My friends leaned in closer and I told them my good, mean idea.

The Bad Baby-sitter

This was my idea: I planned to make Bart look like a bad baby-sitter. By the time Mommy and Seth came home from work, the little house would be one big mess. Mommy and Seth would not be happy about that. They would probably yell at Bart, and then Bart would feel embarrassed.

And I would feel happy again.

On Tuesday afternoon, as soon as Mommy left Andrew and me with Bart, I said, "Let's go outside."

Bart grinned at me. "You are going to play with us today, Karen? That is great. I'm glad to have you back."

I nodded. "First let's have a snack, though. Can we make chocolate milk?"

"Sure," replied Bart.

I took a carton of milk out of the refrigerator. Then I got out glasses, a spoon, and the chocolate powder. "Okay. Here goes," I said. I poured the milk into the glasses. (I sloshed it over the table.) Then I dumped some chocolate into each glass (and over the table). Then I stirred up the chocolate milk. (I left the sticky spoon on the table.)

While Bart wiped off the table, Andrew and I drank our milk. And — *uh-oh* — I spilled mine. Chocolate milk ran down my shirt and onto the floor. "Oops," I said.

"Hey," said Andrew. "I know. Instead of going outside, can we bake a cake? Please, Bart?"

"Yeah, can we?" I asked.

"I don't know," replied Bart. He had just cleaned up the table. Now the floor was a mess. "Karen, go upstairs and change your shirt. I will think about the cake," he said.

"Sorry about the mess, Bart," I called as I ran out of the kitchen. "Here, let me put my shirt in the washing mach — uh-oh."

"Now what?" cried Bart.

"Um, I just spilled the laundry detergent."

"Bart! Someone is at the door!" shouted Andrew from the hallway.

"I'll answer it!" I shouted back.

Kathryn and Willie were on the stoop. They ran inside with their snowy wet clothes on. They left footprints from the front door all the way to the kitchen.

"We are going to bake a cake," I told them, even though Bart had not said we could bake the cake.

"*I* am going to bake it in my bathing suit," said Andrew.

"Why?" I asked.

"In case I spill. I will not have to change my shirt. And I can take a bath with my bathing suit on."

An hour later, the cake was finished. It was a chocolate cake. Bart said there was so much frosting on the floor, he wondered how we had enough left over for the cake. Then he sent Kathryn and Willie home.

"Yikes," said Bart. "It is almost six o'clock."

"Boy, what a mess," I added, looking around the house.

"Hey, Andrew! Do not leave the kitchen before you — " Bart began to say. Too late. Andrew flashed by in his tropical fish bathing suit. He was covered with chocolate. Bart ran after him into the hall. I ran after Bart. And as Bart ran by the plant stand, I knocked it over. I just reached out and — *clunk* — knocked it over.

Bart could not catch it in time. Miss Fern crashed to the floor. Her pot smashed. A leg fell off the plant stand.

"I don't believe it," said Bart. "I finally knocked it over."

I glanced behind me at the chocolatey kitchen. I looked into the powdery laundry room. Then I looked at the hallway, with its dirty snow puddles, the broken plant stand, and the dirt balls and pieces of pottery.

The doorbell rang.

15

You're Fired

A palm tree was standing on our porch. Honest. Bart opened the door, and there was a giant palm tree. A man's face peeked out of the top of the trunk. Sprouting from his head were palm fronds with coconuts.

"Good evening," said the tree.

"Aughhh!" shrieked Andrew. "A talking tree!"

"No, Andrew," I said. "It is a man *dressed* like a tree. . . . Isn't it?" I asked Bart.

"Yup," agreed Bart. He was holding poor Miss Fern in one hand, and the leg from the plant stand in the other.

The palm tree smiled. "Congratulations!" he said. "Karen Brewer has won the Winter Blahs Trip to Bermuda. Is she at home?"

Bart grinned. "Hey, this isn't such a bad day after all. Karen, you won a trip!" Bart turned to the palm tree. "That's Karen," he added, pointing at me. (He pointed with Miss Fern.)

The palm tree frowned. "That cannot be Karen Brewer," he said. "Contestants must be eighteen or older. She is not eighteen."

I had been all set to jump up and down, and cry, "I won! I won! I won!" (I still wanted to go to Bermuda, even if I would not go with Bart.) Instead I said, "Um, you must mean Mommy."

"Karen," said Bart, "he could not mean your mother. Your mother is named Lisa. You are the only Karen Brewer here."

I glared at Bart. "Bart — " I said.

But I was interrupted. Mommy and Seth came home then. They came into the house through the garage door. When they en-

tered the front hallway, they stopped. They stood still. They looked around at the messy house. They looked at Andrew in his bathing suit. They looked at the palm tree at the door. They looked at the broken plant stand, and Bart holding Miss Fern.

"What is going on here?" asked Seth.

Everyone turned toward Seth and Mommy.

"Are you Karen Brewer?" the palm tree asked Mommy.

"No. I am her mother," replied Mommy.

"Then I am afraid we cannot give her the prize. It will have to go to someone else. I'm sorry, Miss Brewer."

I was still glaring at Bart. And now Mommy was glaring at me.

"I entered a contest," I tried to explain. "The palm tree came to tell me I won the grand prize. A trip to Bermuda. But now he won't give it to me. That is not fair."

"Contestants are supposed to be at least eighteen years old," the tree said to Mommy.

74

"What on earth happened here today?" Seth asked Bart.

"Well," began Bart, "we had a few accidents. And then — and then I ran into the plant stand. I am really sorry. I do not know exactly how it happened. But Miss Fern fell on the floor, and . . . I will pay for everything," Bart went on. "I think Miss Fern is okay. She just needs a new pot."

"And a new stand," I added.

Mommy sighed. "We appreciate the offer. I have to ask you not to come back, though, Bart. We will find another baby-sitter."

"Do you mean Bart is fired?" I asked.

"I am afraid so," answered Seth.

"I better be going," said the palm tree.

"Why is Andrew in his bathing suit?" asked Seth.

No one answered him. Bart just said he was sorry again. Then he left.

I was still angry. But a little tiny part of me wanted to smile.

16

Trouble

On Wednesday our new baby-sitter arrived. It was Kristy! Mommy had said the new sitter would be a nice surprise, and she was right.

"So what do you guys want to do this afternoon?" Kristy asked Andrew and me after Mommy had left.

Andrew shrugged his shoulders. But I knew what I wanted to do. "Nancy is coming over today," I replied. "We are going to make valentines."

Sure enough, a few minutes later the

doorbell rang. Nancy came inside carrying a bag of stuff. The stuff was for our valentines — ribbons and buttons and bits of lace. And of course red paper. We were going to look through my collage box, too.

Nancy and I went upstairs. Kristy and Andrew stayed downstairs. They were going to make a city out of Legos.

"Karen," said Nancy when we were sitting at the table in my room. "Tell me again why you cannot go to Bermuda."

I sighed. "Because Bart ruined my trip. I could have won it. They had drawn *my* name for the grand prize. But the winner is supposed to be eighteen."

"Why?" asked Nancy.

"I don't know. I do not understand. Anyway, I tried to say that *Mommy* is Karen Brewer, since she is more than eighteen. But Bart kept pointing at *me*. So the palm tree knew. And he took my prize away to give to somebody else. Mean old Bart."

"Yeah, mean old Bart," agreed Nancy.

Nancy and I worked quietly for a few minutes. We were very busy gluing and coloring and cutting things.

Finally I said, "I am *glad* I knocked over that plant stand. I am glad I got Bart in trouble."

"Ahem."

I glanced up. Kristy was standing in the doorway to my room. "*You* knocked over the plant stand, Karen?"

"Well, I — "

"Your mother thinks Bart knocked it over. That is one of the reasons she fired him. Karen, is there anything else I should know about yesterday?"

I looked at Nancy. She was looking at me. "Um," I began to say.

"I think Nancy better go home," Kristy went on.

Nancy stood up. "Okay," she said. She gathered up her valentines and left.

Kristy sat in the chair Nancy had been using. "Karen?" she said.

I sighed. "I was running through the hall

behind Bart," I said. "When he passed the stand, I knocked it over."

"By accident?" asked Kristy.

I shook my head. "No. Because I was mad at Bart."

Kristy was frowning. "Begin at the beginning, Karen. Tell me the whole story."

"All right." I told Kristy everything. I told her about the date and about why I was mad. I told her about the messes I made, and even about entering the contest. "So when Mommy and Seth came home," I finished up, "the house was a mess. Andrew was wearing his bathing suit, Miss Fern had no pot, and a palm tree was at the door."

"Karen, you made those messes on purpose," said Kristy. She looked very serious. "And you knocked the plant stand over on purpose."

"But Bart — " I began.

"Uh-uh," Kristy interrupted me. "Bart did not do anything wrong. He did not know you thought he was asking you for a date. And he did not know about the contest. He was telling the palm tree the truth. You were unfair to Bart, Karen."

I nodded. "I guess so."

"And you will have to tell Seth and your mom what you did."

17

The Honest Truth

I played quietly that afternoon. I worked on my valentines a little. I read a little. But mostly I thought about Bart.

When Mommy and Seth came home, Kristy said to them, "Karen has something to tell you. Don't you, Karen?"

I hung my head. "Yeah."

"It sounds important," said Mommy. "Okay. We will talk about it after dinner when we will not be rushed."

When dinner was over that night, Mommy and Seth and I sat in the living room. We sat in a row on the couch. I sat in the middle.

"All right," said Seth. "Shoot." (He meant start talking.)

I told my story again. I told Mommy and Seth just what I had told Kristy. When I finished, they did not look very happy.

Seth shook his head.

Mommy said, "I cannot believe I *fired* Bart. I feel terrible." Then she said, "Karen, you are in Very Big Trouble."

"I thought so," I replied.

"First of all," began Seth, "you must help us to pay for a new pot for Miss Fern. No allowance for four weeks. I can fix the plant stand myself, though."

"And," said Mommy, "you are grounded for the next two afternoons. When you come home from school, you will go straight to your room and stay there. You may come downstairs for dinner, though."

"Okay," I said. (I really was in Very Big Trouble.)

"Now," Mommy went on, "I am going

to call Bart. I am going to offer his job back to him. He can baby-sit for the last two afternoons. If he wants to. After I have talked to him, I want you to get on the phone, Karen. I want you to apologize. And sound as if you mean it."

"Okay," I said again.

Mommy and I went into the kitchen. Mommy picked up the phone. She told Bart what I had done. Then she said, "And so, Mr. Engle and I would be very happy if you would come back and finish your job here." Bart must have said he would, because then Mommy said, "Oh, that is wonderful. Thank you for understanding. Now I think Karen has something to say to you."

Mommy handed me the phone. "Hi, Bart," I said. "It's me, Karen. I am very, very sorry about the plant stand. I am sorry I got you in trouble, too."

"Okay, Karen," replied Bart. "I will see you tomorrow."

18

Boys and Boyfriends

I was not looking forward to Thursday afternoon. I would be grounded in my room then. Plus, Bart would be our babysitter. I would have to see him. I would have to talk to him. And he was probably mad at me.

When our doorbell rang on Thursday, I could not answer it. I was stuck in my room. Andrew answered it instead. I heard him cry, "Bart! You came back! Can we have the Olympics again?"

"I don't think so," Bart replied. "Karen has to stay inside today."

"Boo," said Andrew.

After Mommy left, Bart came upstairs to see me. "I am sorry you are grounded," he said.

"So am I," added Andrew. "I wanted to play outside."

I stuck my tongue out at Andrew.

Then I said to Bart, "Mommy bought a new pot for Miss Fern today."

"Oh, good," replied Bart. "I was worried about Miss Fern."

"Bart? Are you mad at me?" I asked.

"*I* am," said Andrew. "I *want* to *go* out*side*."

Bart and I both ignored Andrew. Bart looked thoughtful. At last he said, "I am mad at what you did, but I am not mad at you."

I felt a little better after that. Even when Bart and Andrew ran downstairs and left me alone in my room.

Bart was extra, extra neat and careful that

afternoon. He did not let any kids in the house. He cleaned up Andrew's messes right away. He did not allow ball-throwing in the living room. When Mommy and Seth came home, they looked pleased.

"See you tomorrow, Bart!" they called when he left.

After dinner that night, I said to Mommy, "I know I am supposed to stay in my room, but may I please call Kristy? I think I need to apologize to her, too. After all, Bart is her friend. As soon as I have finished, I will go right back to my room. I promise."

"Okay," said Mommy. "You may call Kristy."

I called Kristy from Mommy and Seth's room. I needed privacy. "Kristy," I began, "I want to say I am sorry. Sorry about what I did to Bart."

Kristy sighed. "What you did is not okay. But I am not angry with you. Tell me again why *you* were so angry with *Bart*, though."

"Because he lied about our date."

"But Karen, I do not think Bart asked you for a date. Try to remember what he said to you. What words did he use?"

"He — he invited me over to watch a movie."

"And you *thought* he was asking you for a date."

"I guess so."

"Karen, don't you know that Bart is *my* boyfriend?"

"Is he really?"

"Well, yes. Also — Karen, did you really think Bart was asking a seven-year-old for a date? Bart is thirteen."

"I didn't think about that."

"Boys and boyfriends can be confusing," said Kristy. "There is a lot to think about — crushes and dating."

"And getting married," I added. "I am married to Ricky Torres."

"But you know that is just for play. Don't you?" asked Kristy. "Seven-year-olds do not *really* date. And they certainly do not *really* get married. Boyfriends and dating are serious, grown-up things. Wait until you are ready for them, Karen."

"I will," I said. "But Kristy, sometimes I just want to be older."

"And you will be," said Kristy. "But for now, enjoy being seven."

19

Bart's Present

By Friday, I felt a little better. But I was still grounded. I could not leave my room. Bart came to see me as soon as Mommy had left. This time he said, "Karen, your mother told me I could take Andrew outside today as long as we stay in the yard. That way, you can see us from your windows. If you need anything, you can call to me."

"Okay," I said.

I listened as Bart helped Andrew get ready to play in the snow. "When you want

90

to come inside," Bart said, "take off your boots first. No walking around the house in them. And take off your other things by the door. I will hang them up for you. I do not want puddles in the house. And if your mittens are very wet . . ."

The door slammed.

I looked out my window. I watched Bart and Andrew carry the toboggan to the sledding track.

Then I turned away. I sat at my table. Ms. Colman had told us to finish a page in our reading workbook. So I did. After that I got out my collage. Maybe I could finish it. I looked at what I had done so far. The paper was very full. But the collage was not quite right. I added some of the wood shavings I had found at Seth's workshop. Then I wrote some words on the paper. Did you know that words can be part of a collage? Well, they can. I wrote

HAPPY

on the collage. Then I turned the paper sideways. I wrote

SEASONS

near a corner. Finally I added

PEOPLE

near another corner. My collage was finished at last.

I stood up. Where should I hang my beautiful collage? I could not decide. I stepped over to the window. I leaned on the sill and looked into the yard. Willie and Kathryn had come over. They were sledding with Bart and Andrew. I let out a little sigh. I still felt bad about what had happened to Bart. He had been fired from his first big baby-sitting job, and it was all my fault.

I wished I could do something nice for Bart. Maybe . . .

I ran to my desk. I found my best writing paper. Usually, I only use it for thank-you notes to my grandparents. I wrote:

DEAR BART,

I KNOW I ALREADY TOLD YOU I AM SORRY. BUT I AM GOING TO SAY IT AGAIN. I AM VERY, VERY, VERY, VERY, VERY, VERY SORRY FOR ALL THE MEAN THINGS I DID. I HOPE WE CAN STILL BE F~~REI FOR~~ FRIENDS. I MADE THIS PRESENT FOR YOU. IT IS A COLA COOL COLLAGE. I WORKED ON IT FOR A LONG TIME. IN CASE YOU CANNOT TELL, IT IS A PICTURE ABOUT SEASONS AND PEOPLE AND HAPPY TIMES.

LOVE, KAREN

P.S. I HOPE YOU CAN STILL BABY-SIT FOR ANDREW AND ME SOMETIMES.

I gave the present to Bart when he and Andrew came inside later. "It is a collage,"

I told him. "I want you to have it. You are one of the best baby-sitters Andrew and I have ever had."

Bart was silent for a few moments. He studied the collage. Then he smiled at me. "Thank you, Karen," he said. "I am sorry we had a misunderstanding. But I want to be friends, too. I will always keep the collage."

The Date

Bart's baby-sitting job was over. Ruth was back at work in Seth's office. Her mother was all better. Mommy was at home in the afternoons again. And I was finished being grounded.

One evening, Kristy called me from the big house.

"Hi, Karen," she said. "How are you?"

"Fine," I answered. "But I miss you and Daddy and my big-house family. I will see you this weekend, though."

"I know. That is why I am calling. Bart

and I have a date on Saturday afternoon. We want to know if you would like to come with us. Just the three of us. Maybe it will make up a little bit for the awful date. Bart and I still feel bad about that. What do you think?"

"Come on a date with you and Bart?" I replied.

"Yes. Not a boyfriend-girlfriend date. I mean, *Bart* and *I* are the boyfriend and girl-friend. But we want *you* to come along for a special day."

"Okay!" I cried. "Sure! Thank you, Kristy."

Our date began after lunch on Saturday. Kristy had said I did not have to get dressed up. But I wanted to look nice. I wore my blue jean skirt, a turtleneck shirt with red hearts on it, white tights, flop socks, and a pair of new sneakers.

"How do I look?" I asked Kristy.

"Perfect," she replied. "Let's go." (Kristy was wearing jeans and a sweat shirt. That is just about the only outfit she ever wears.)

Charlie drove Kristy and me downtown in the Junk Bucket. (That is his car.) He let us out in front of the movie theater. Bart was waiting for us there. " 'Bye, kids!" called Charlie. "Have fun."

"We are not kids!" Kristy shouted after him. (Charlie did not hear her.)

I looked up at the sign over the movie theater. *"Homeward Bound,"* I read.

Bart was smiling at me. "Do you know what it's about, Karen? It is a new version of *The Incredible Journey*. It is the same story about the two dogs and the cat who travel across the country. Kristy and I figured you did not pay much attention to the video at my house. We thought you might like to try the story again, now that you can enjoy it."

"Thank you, thank you, thank you!" I exclaimed.

Bart and Kristy and I bought tickets. We crowded into the theater. I was the only kid there who was not with an adult. I felt very grown-up. We sat in the first row of the balcony. Bart and Kristy let me sit between them. We were smack in the middle of the theater.

"Best seats in the house," said Bart.

The movie began. Bart was right. I had not paid any attention to the video at his house. The story was very exciting. Some parts were funny, and some were sad, too. I sat on the edge of my seat. (I think Bart and Kristy held hands behind me.)

When the movie was over, I blew my nose. Then I wiped my eyes. "That was soooo good," I said. I paused. "Is our date over?"

"Not yet," replied Kristy.

Kristy and Bart and I walked to the Rosebud Cafe. We sat at a booth. We ordered sodas and a plate of French fries. This was not a healthy snack, but I did not care. I had seen a great movie. I was with Kristy and Bart. And nobody was angry at anyone else.

I sighed.

"Karen? What is wrong?" asked Kristy.

"Nothing," I replied. "I am happy. Thank you for inviting me on your date."

About the Author

ANN M. MARTIN lives in New York City and loves animals, especially cats. She has two cats of her own, Mouse and Rosie.

Other books by Ann M. Martin that you might enjoy are *Stage Fright*; *Me and Katie (the Pest)*; and the books in *The Baby-sitters Club* series.

Ann likes ice cream and *I Love Lucy*. And she has her own little sister, whose name is Jane.

Little Sister

Don't miss #47

KAREN'S KITE

"Soon you will get a chance to make a kite of your own," said Mr. Mackey. "And that's not all. We will hold a kite-flying contest. You will get to stay after school on a Friday and fly your kites on the playground. Then we will have a school sleepover so we can watch the kites fly all night. Whoever builds the kite that stays up the longest wins the contest."

"Yipee!" "Cool!" "Neat!" Everyone was calling out at once. Mr. Mackey held up his hand for quiet.

"Before you begin making your kites, we'll take a trip to Mrs. Moody's Kite Store. Mrs. Moody will tell us about the different kites she sells."

I could hardly wait.

BABY-SITTERS™
Little Sister
by Ann M. Martin
author of The Baby-sitters Club®

More Titles... ➡

The Baby-sitters Little Sister titles continued...

- -

Available wherever you buy books, or use this order form.

Scholastic Inc., P.O. Box 7502, Jefferson City, MO 65102

Please send me the books I have checked above. I am enclosing $_____
(please add $2.00 to cover shipping and handling). Send check or money order – no
cash or C.O.Ds please.

Name_____ Birthdate_____

Address_____

City_____State/Zip_____

Please allow four to six weeks for delivery. Offer good in U.S.A. only. Sorry, mail orders are not
available to residents to Canada. Prices subject to change.   BSLS497